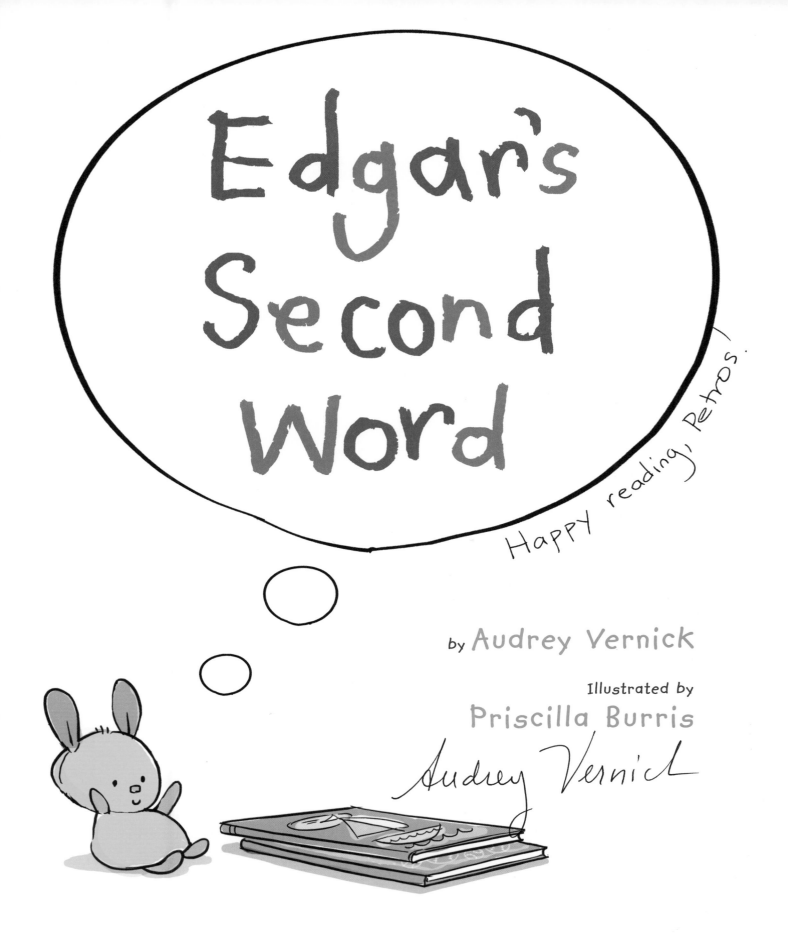

Edgar's Second Word

Happy reading, Petros.

by Audrey Vernick

Illustrated by
Priscilla Burris

Audrey Vernick

CLARION BOOKS • Houghton Mifflin Harcourt • Boston   New York

THE books Hazel planned to read to her someday-brother waited on a special shelf.

Every night, she imagined the warm-love weight of him on her lap, and how they'd study each page together.

She read to her bunny, Rodrigo, but it wasn't the same.

When Edgar finally came along, Hazel celebrated.

But Edgar wasn't much different from Rodrigo.

Or a pillow.

Or a watermelon.

Hazel went back to waiting.

As Mom noted Edgar's firsts in the Baby Book, Hazel waited for the first that *mattered*.

Edgar's first word.

Hazel read Edgar stories, but she didn't know if he understood.

She wished he would whisper questions.

But Edgar didn't speak.

Mostly, he pointed.

And grunted.

Like a pointing, grunting watermelon.

Then—finally!—it happened! Edgar said his first word!
Mom reached for the Baby Book. Hazel cheered.
Then Edgar said his first word again.
He said it with force. With meaning. With conviction!

NO!

Edgar roared.

Hazel thought of all they
could finally do now that Edgar
was talking.

"Want to play school?"
she asked.

"NO!"

"Store?"

"No!"

"Let's play with your farm."

"NO!"

"How about your squeaky-honky-quacky duck?" (Hazel hated the squeaky-honky-quacky duck. But she was desperate.)

Edgar shoved his head against Hazel's leg like a ram from some kind of angry-animal farm.

"Change of scenery!" Mom called.

"Choose some books, Edgar," Hazel said.

"Want to do a puzzle?"

Edgar's "NO!" was so loud that people stared. Some covered their ears. A librarian fainted.

Mom quickly realized, though perhaps not quickly enough, that a library wasn't the best place for a *NO*-shouting boy. They checked out *books* and returned home.

"Let's have a tea party with Rodrigo," Hazel said.

Hazel was ready to scream.
The rabbit, however, looked relieved.

"When *you're* a mother," Hazel's mother said, "you'll agree there's nothing sweeter than hearing your baby talk for the first time."

Hazel did not agree.

She had waited forever for Edgar.

Then another forever for Edgar to talk.

"It's not sweet if he's grouchy," Hazel muttered.

"And mean. And angry-sounding. And growly."

"NO!" Edgar said. "NO, NO, NO, NO!"
"Why, Edgar," Mom said, reaching for the Baby Book,
"I believe you just said your first sentence."

Hazel wanted to hiss and kick and spit like an extremely annoyed llama. Instead, she smiled a big, fake smile. "Let's learn some new words, yes?" She showed Edgar how to say the word—first smile, then *y*, then *es*. "YES? Yes? YYYYYYYYYES?"

Go ahead and guess how Edgar replied.

Hazel imagined Edgar's future.
"Want to share my shovel?"

"Edgar, would you please read aloud?"

"Uncle Edgar, will you come on the roller coaster with us?"

The day's *no*'s added up.
Everyone was tired.
Finally, it was bedtime.

Hazel reached for her *no*-saying grump of a brother.
Edgar got as far as "Nnn" before a tired-baby gravity
settled him on her lap.

Edgar felt as weighty as two Edgars.

He leaned back, a heavy-headed, warmly cuddled,
not-*no*-saying lamb of a ram.

Hazel began to read.

When she turned the very last page, it was quiet. So quiet, they wondered if Edgar had drifted to sleep.

That was when Edgar said his second word:

Again-

In the stunned silence of the room, Edgar tried out his third word, too.

"Again," Hazel said.

The End

For the original Edgar and his mom, Julia, an excellent sharer
—A.V.

For two wise and wonderful moms, Lily Garcia and Harriet Burris—
I am *so* grateful for you. —P.B.

Clarion Books, 215 Park Avenue South, New York, New York 10003 • Text copyright © 2014 by Audrey Vernick • Illustrations copyright © 2014 by Priscilla Burris • All rights reserved. For information about permission to reproduce selections from this book, write to Permissions, Houghton Mifflin Harcourt Publishing Company, 215 Park Avenue South, New York, New York 10003. • Clarion Books is an imprint of Houghton Mifflin Harcourt Publishing Company. • www.hmhbooks.com • The illustrations in this book were executed digitally. • The text was set in Kidprint. • Design by Sharismar Rodriguez • Library of Congress Cataloging-in-Publication Data • Vernick, Audrey. • Edgar's second word / by Audrey Vernick ; illustrated by Priscilla Burris. • p. cm. • Summary: After waiting for her baby brother to arrive, and then waiting for him to learn to talk, Hazel is disappointed in his first word. • ISBN 978-0-547-68462-8 (hardcover) • [1. Conversation—Fiction. 2. Babies—Fiction. 3. Brothers—Fiction.] I. Burris, Priscilla, ill. II. Title. • PZ7.V5973Edg 2014 • [E]—dc23 • 2011052435 • Manufactured in China • SCP 10 9 8 7 6 5 4 3 2 1
4500459796